The Day that Falsehood Sought to be King

Author

Fuad A. Kamal

Illustrator

Piotr Antoniak

O nce upon a time, Truth ("Pen") and Falsehood ("Cloak of Darkness & Illusions") went for a walk...

...and had a heated argument about the value of truth for a village called Wealth. Falsehood (also known as "Cloak of Fancies"), tried hard to present an opposite view of the facts to Truth, at one time even suggesting a tree was upside-down when it was, in fact, upright.

So Truth and Falsehood went before Justice ("Weighty Boulder") to present their case. Falsehood told Justice, "Give me a day, and I will have the village of Wealth under my grip."

Justice responded, "I will let the village decide who and what they value."

Falsehood wasted no time in coming up with a plan.

The next day, Falsehood approached one of village chiefs, Chief Knot Bookish, and told him that one of the other village chiefs, Chief Forte R. Uss, was plotting to destroy him and to take over.

Knot Bookish was so agitated that the chief neglected to notice Falsehood's presence had distorted the image of the clock on the wall.

Chief Knot Bookish rushed out to investigate with a sword in hand but with hardly a question asked.

Reckless? Not particularly for people from the village group to which he belonged. Many from that group had long ago given in to the comfort of shallow, hollow thoughts. After all, why disturb a self-satisfied existence with annoying questions?

So the chief wildly waved his sword while proudly wearing a ridiculously tall, hollow hat, which was sadly empty of any facts. He then pursued his imaginary foe with a mix of wide-eyed enthusiasm and a level of rigor that was quite unusual for him.

"Did you know that the chief is coming to harm you with his sword?" Fear ("Licking Flame"), Falsehood's travel companion, asked one of his supposed rivals ("Chief Forte R. Uss"). "You better be ready for him!" said Fear, burning brightly.

Chief Forte R. Uss immediately picked up his sword. In light of the blinding blaze put out by Fear, the rival selected a gloriously tall hat that both clouded and protected his vision. Thus, Forte R. Uss neglected to notice that Falsehood's robe was selective in the light that it let pass through, and that Falsehood blocked or hid bits and pieces of the truth.

The two village groups quickly fell upon each other. Unfortunately, this caused the remaining village groups to be sucked into the battle.

Falsehood spent the rest of the day marveling and chuckling at the success of his underhanded plan. (He had been confident that almost any of the schemes from his trusty bag of tricks would probably have worked for the village.)

By the end of the day, the Battle of the Tall, Stumbling Hats (as it came to be known) had finished, and Falsehood was victorious. Clearly, the village had fallen to him.

Falsehood approached Justice and asked him for the village.

Truth was quiet and looked tiny before a now towering and gloating Falsehood.

Justice was forced to give the village to Falsehood, and falsehood took command of the land. And so it came that Falsehood, a summoner of fantastic fantasies, rose to the throne of the land.

Disappointed, Justice and Truth could only look at each other in quiet desperation.

As time passed, the prosperous village became poor. Many lies and distortions that were once internal to Falsehood, spread like a sickness into the core of the village.

Streams flowed with a toxic, green slime. Parts of the sky randomly blotted out. Trees grew oddly, overturned from the sky. Parts of the village lost their color and turned into a mixture of black and white. Even creepy pop-up boxes grew and lurked in the corners.

However, as the village steadily decayed, Falsehood began to lose interest in commanding a declining empire.

At this time, Hope ("Daisy Smilesalot") and Youth ("Energy Del Sneakers") visited Truth and asked him, "Why have you stood still and not said anything?"

"No one wanted me," replied Truth.

"We want you!" replied Hope and Youth. With those three magical words, Truth grew ten feet taller.

"Let us help you confront Falsehood," said Hope and Youth to Truth.

Justice barely managed to suppress a widening smile.

Then Truth grew twenty feet taller. What a difference it makes when people believe and value something strongly!

Falsehood, who was actually quite lazy, took one look at the now towering figure of Truth and fled.

"Who needs the bother of this moth-eaten, rotten village anyway?" Falsehood declared, as he made a hasty retreat.

As Truth glowed, the village's weeds were replaced by fruit trees. The stagnant water could now be seen as brilliant waterfalls and flowing, crystal-clear streams.

Ice cream hills and flying lollipop delights dotted the landscape. Sunshine plants and heart-shaped flowers filled the fields. Money grew on trees. Joy filled the village.

With Truth in charge, the village of Wealth became a place where many different types of wealth could blossom.

Justice was pleased with the new king.

Wisdom ("The Grand Old Tree"), Truth's uncle, said, "Falsehood is very powerful, but he can only conquer with darkness. The more powerful he becomes, the more he will devour all light around him, destroying everything. Finally, he consumes himself. Only Truth can truly rule over the real soul of Wealth, in its many wonderful forms."

"Wealth has found its true king!" Justice declared.

If you liked this book, check out some other books by the author:

Website: www.fuadakamal.com